COYOTE &
LITTLE TURTLE

IISAW NIQW YÖNGÖSONHOYA A TRADITIONAL HOPI TALE

DEAREST CHEYENNE:
THIS WILL HELP YOU REMEMBER
OUR FIRST MEETING —
LOVE YOU
UNCLE BILLY + AUNT ECANE

BASED ON A STORY
TOLD BY
HERSHEL TALASHOEMA

TRANSLATED
& EDITED BY
**EMORY SEKAQUAPTEWA &
BARBARA PEPPER**

ILLUSTRATED BY
HOPI CHILDREN

CLEAR LIGHT PUBLISHERS
SANTA FE, NEW MEXICO

IT IS HOT

COYOTE &
LITTLE TURTLE

IISAW NIQW YÖNGÖSONHOYA
A TRADITIONAL HOPI TALE

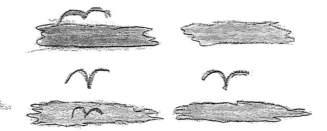

Clear Light Publishers, 823 Don Diego, Santa Fe, New Mexico 87501

Clear Light Publishers' Original Language Series, IPOLA Imprint
Bilingual Hopi-English edition with glossary

LIBRARY OF CONGRESS CATALOGING-IN-PUBLICATION DATA

Coyote & Little Turtle: Iisaw Niqw Yöngösonhoya: A traditional Hopi tale / translated and edited by Emory Sekaquaptewa & Barbara Pepper, based on a story told by Herschel Talashoema : illustrated by Hopi children.— 1st ed.
      p.   cm.
Bilingual Hopi-English edition with glossary.
ISBN 0-940666-85-5 (pbk.) : $ 9.95
1. Hopi Indians—Legends. 2. Coyote (Legendary character)—Legends. [1. Hopi Indians—Legends. 2. Indians of North America—Legends. 3. Coyote (Legendary character)—Legends. 4. Hopi language materials—Bilingual.] I. Sekaquaptewa, Emory. II. Pepper, Barbara, 1949- . III. Talashoema, Herschel. IV. Title: Coyote and Little Turtle. V. Title: Iisaw Niqw Yöngösonhoya.
E99.H7C67 1993
398.24'52974442—dc20   93-21393
                                          CIP
                                             AC
The materials in this publication have been developed at the Hotevilla-Bacavi Community School in collaboration with and sponsored by IPOLA.

IPOLA, The Institute for the Preservation of the Original Languages of the Americas is a 501 (c) (3) foundation located at 1237 Cerro Gordo, Santa Fe, New Mexico, 87501.

First Edition   10 9 8 7 6 5 4 3 2

DEDICATION

"The dream of preservation of the Hopi language through Hopi stories for the Hopi children will be the survival of the Hopi culture for future generations."

Le Roy N. Shingoitewa, School Principal, Hotevilla-Bacavi Community School when this book was being created

"I am honored to be involved and part of this project for the Hopi children."
"Nuy qa peevewnayaqw nu' nùutumniikyangw Hopitsatsakwmuy amungem it tutuvenyukit tumàltaqe amungem hàalayti."

Storyteller, Herschel Talashoema

"The Hopi language is the heart of our culture. We must never forsake it. This book is a testament to the Hopi's resolve to preserve our birthright."

Leigh Jenkins, Director, Hopi Cultural Preservation Office

THANK YOU!
ASKWALI!

To the **students**, **staff**, **library committee**, the **Board of the Hotevilla-Bacavi School**; the **storytellers**, **PTA**, and the **community of Hotevilla-Bacavi** for their patience and support; **Le Roy Shingoitewa**, Principal, who initiated this pilot project for IPOLA; **Leigh Jenkins**, Director, Hopi Cultural Preservation Office (IPOLA Board member); **Merwin Kooyahoema**, the Hopi Tribe video technician, and **Michael Bond**, Director for the storytelling video complementing this book.

Dr. Carlos Vélez-Ibáñez and the **Bureau of Applied Research in Anthropology** (B.A.R.A.) at the **University of Arizona** under his supervision, for their guidance and efforts to bring this project to fruition, and for their ongoing dedication and commitment, not only to the Hopi storybooks, but to IPOLA. **Emory Sekaquaptewa**, B.A.R.A., University of Arizona, for his dedication to preserving the Hopi language with his work on the Hopi Dictionary Project.

Barbara Pepper, translator and editor, for her dedication to this project; **Mary Black**, B.A.R.A., Hopi Dictionary Project, for her help with editing; **Eugene Sekaquaptewa**, Field Producer for the Hopi Storybook Project, mentor, and liaison between IPOLA and the community.

Deryck Healey, **Judy Herzl**, **Alexandra Hess**, and **Kosta Galinis** for their artistic contribution; and **Donald Hess** for his enthusiasm and continuing support.

In this book you will find

INTRODUCTION

The following story was told in the Hopi language by Herschel Talashoema (Talashoyiwma). It is offered here as an example of how each traditional story in the forthcoming series of children's Hopi storybooks will look.

As each of these stories was told, it was also videotaped. The stories often took as long as ten minutes to tell, and therefore were rather lengthy when they were translated word for word.

And so, as we felt that the children needed a more simplistic version, in order to hold their interest and to facilitate their eventual reading, we condensed the stories with the storytellers' permission into these shorter versions, one example of which is this first storybook.

Each story was listened to from the original tape recording and translated into English sentence by sentence. Then the story was read through and shortened as much as possible, still trying to keep the original intent and personality of the storyteller.

Once the story was in short English sentences, then those sentences were translated back into Hopi, again trying to use much of the original vocabulary that the storyteller used.

We hope that you will enjoy reading the shortened versions, and that your children will be able not only to learn the stories so that they may one day be able to pass them on, but also one day be able to read them in the Hopi language.

Joe Gebhardt

Jennifer Canyon
(Leposmana)

Dusty Brown
(Posiwhoya)

Bensita Komaquaptewa
(Tephongqa)

Kevin Cooper
(Kyelhoynaya)

Lloyd Frank

Dan Gebhardt

Deldrick Poleahla
(Maavuyawma)

Orval Elliot
(Pusumti)

Adam Kyasyousie
(Puhuwari)

The Illustrators

Grades kindergarten through sixth

Duran Howato
(Pisa)

Jerel Qumahongnewa
(Naa' itnaya)

Blayne Honani
(Piphepwisa)

Lori Monongye
(Talasmana)

Curtis Yowytewa
(Kuyvawisa)

Merle Calnimptewa
(Hoohu)

Hopi names are in parentheses

Tracy Cuch
(Piva' inmana)

Katherine Kinale
(Nata' aska)

LouEllen Nutumya
(Sa' lakwmana)

Cindi Howato
(Tawayesnöm)

Robyna Bilagody
(Tawasimana)

Cassandra Kinale
(Kyaromana)

Jared Honanwaima
(Wupnaya)

Marvis Lomayestewa
(Taqahonaw)

Corey Ahownewa
(Paaqavi)

Leif Kootswatewa
(Muuyawhoya)

Darrell Calnimptewa
(Yeeva)

Nicole Honanie
(Pipwaysi)

Shana Koiyumptewa
(Polimana)

Curtis Lomayahtewa
(Tsavatawa)

Andrea Salazar
(Pipmana)

Garrett Lomatska
(A' nihoya)

Yaw Orayve yeesiwa.

Everyone was living at Oraibi.

Yöngösosont Leenangwvat ep ki'yyungwa.

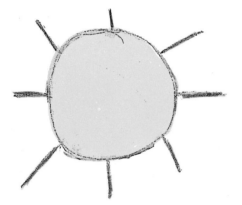

Sutsep iits talavay Yöngösosont

 tunöshepnumyangwu.

The Turtles lived near Leenangwva.

Early each morning the Turtles went

looking for food.

Yaw Iisaw Ismo'walpe ki'yta.

Sutsep talavay Iisaw maqnumngwu.

12

Now, Coyote lived at Ismo'wala.

Coyote also went hunting each morning.

Pu' hisat talavay Yöngösosont

tunöshepnumya.

Noqw sùutala'niqw,

oovi a'ni (hin'ur) kotskiwa.

14

Now, one morning the Turtles

were out looking for food.

Since it was midsummer,

the sand was very hot.

Yaw suukya Yöngösonhoya
puwmoki.

Pam pòöpangaqw lasqe, pam
himutskit àasonmiq paki.
Pam puwvaqw, kur sòosoyam
Yöngösosont ninma.

16

One Little Turtle became sleepy.

He went off the path and under a bush.

The other Turtles went on home

without him when he went to sleep.

Yaw Yöngösonhoya nawis'ew taatayi.

"Ya puma haqamiya ?" pam yan wuuwa.
Pam as pumuy kuk.wuwàaqe
        amungkniqw a'ni (hin'ur) kotskiwa.

Yaw Yöngösonhoya paklawu:

Tingawsona, tingawsona, tingawsona, tingawsona
Wa'ooo, wa'ooo,
Hi, hi, hi, hi !

18

Little Turtle finally woke up.

"Where did they go ?" he wondered.
He tried to follow their tracks,
but the sand was too hot.

Little Turtle began to cry:

Tingawsona, tingawsona, tingawsona, tingawsona
Wa'ooo, wa'ooo,
Hi, hi, hi, hi !

21

Pam posvalweheheta.
Noqw yaw Iisaw kur aqle' haqe' maqnuma.

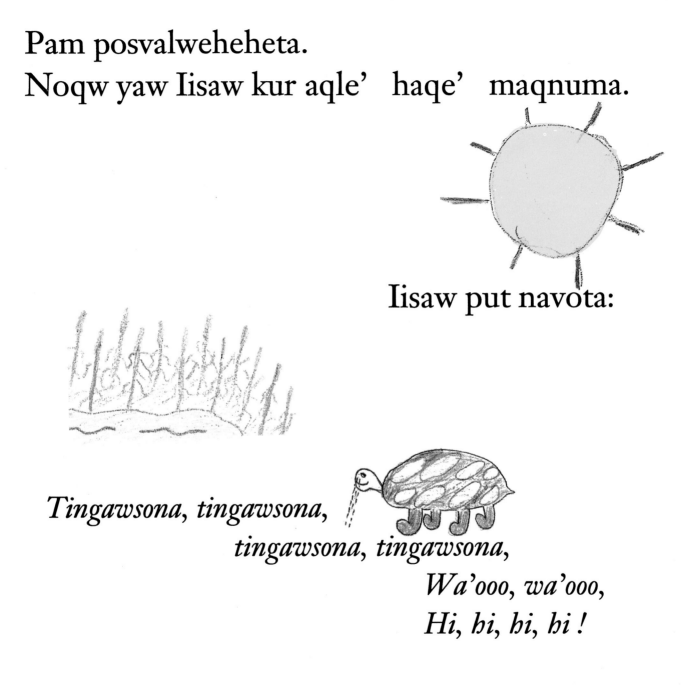

Iisaw put navota:

Tingawsona, tingawsona,
    tingawsona, tingawsona,
        Wa'ooo, wa'ooo,
        Hi, hi, hi, hi !

He was bathed in tears.

It so happened that Coyote was
hunting somewhere nearby.

Coyote heard the crying:

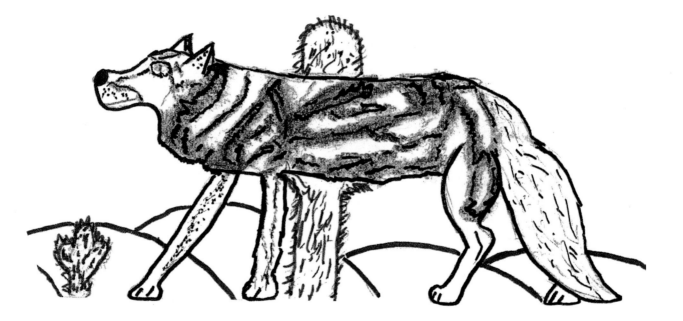

Tingawsona, tingawsona, tingawsona, tingawsona
Wa'ooo, wa'ooo,
Hi, hi, hi, hi !

"Ya himu haqam hìngqawlawu ?"

Iisaw yan wuuwa.

Piw pam put navota:

Tingawsona, tingawsona, tingawsona, tingawsona
Wa'ooo, wa'ooo,
Hi, hi, hi, hi !

"What could be making such a noise ?"

Coyote wondered.

Again he heard it:

Tingawsona, tingawsona, tingawsona, tingawsona
Wa'ooo, wa'ooo,
Hi, hi, hi, hi !

Pàasat pam Yöngösonhoyat himutskit
àasonngaqw tuwa.

"Ya um hìita tawlawuy ?" Iisaw kita.

"Nu' qa tawlawu, nu' pakmumuya,"
                                    Yöngösonhoya kita.

Then he saw Little Turtle under a bush.
   "What are you singing ?" asked Coyote.

"I wasn't singing, I was crying,"
                said Little Turtle.

"Piw tawlawu'u !" Iisaw kita.

"Hep nu' qa tawlawu, nu' pakmumuya,"

Yöngösonhoya kita.

"Sing again !" Coyote said.

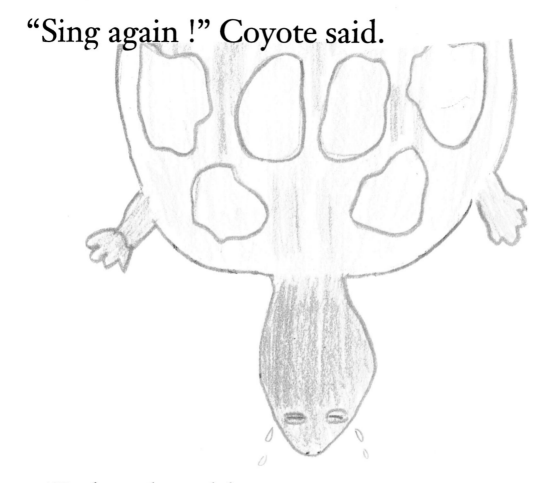

"I already told you, I wasn't singing,

I was crying," Little Turtle said.

"Um inumi qa tawlawqw, pu' nu' ung
Nuvatukya'oviy ep nuvat ang muumaniy,"
Iisaw kita.

"Taa'awu, taa'awu, nu' nuvat akw
qa hìntingwu," Yöngösonhoya kita.

"If you don't sing for me, I'll take you up
to Nuvatukya'ovi and roll you in the snow,"
Coyote said.

"That's OK, that's OK, snow doesn't
bother me," Little Turtle said.

Pàasat pu' yaw Iisaw piw wuuwanlawu.
"Um inumi qa tawlawqw, nu' ung
kotskiwqat ang muumaniy," Iisaw kita.

"Taa'awu, taa'awu,"
Yöngösonhoya kita. "Nu' tuuwat natuwi'yta."

Coyote thought some more.

"If you don't sing for me, I'll tumble you in the hot sand," Coyote said.

"That's OK, that's OK," Little Turtle said.

"I'm used to sand."

PÀASAT Iisaw itsivuti.

"Um inumi qa tawlawqw, nu' ung

Leenangwvami wiikye' ung aqw

tuuvani," Iisaw kita.

NOW Coyote was really getting mad.

"If you don't sing for me, I'll take you to Leenangwva and throw you in," Coyote said.

"So'ni, so'ni," yaw Yöngösonhoya kita.
"Nu' pànte', nu' sumokni."

Pu' Iisaw put

sùukyàatsantat pu'

Leenangwvat aw wari.

"Oh, no o o o ! " said Little Turtle.
"If that happens to me, I' ll die."

Coyote quickly

grabbed Little Turtle in his mouth

and ran to Leenangwva.

37

Yaw Iisaw Leenangwvat ep pitut, pam
Yöngösonhoyat paamiq tuuva.

Okiw Yöngösonhoya atkyamiq pakima.

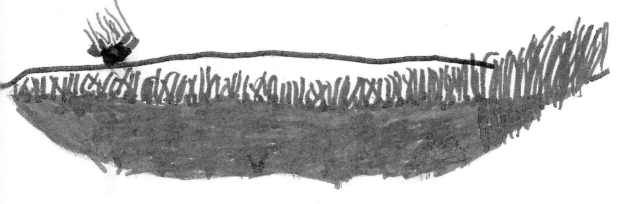

When Coyote arrived at Leenangwva, he hurled Little Turtle into the water.

Little Turtle sank way down, poor thing.

Pu' pàasat, Iisaw taytaqw,
Yöngösonhoya ahoy kuyva !!

"Is ali !" Yöngösonhoya Iisawuy aqw yan

töqti. "Nu' yangqw ki'yta."

Ha Ha

But then, while Coyote was watching,
Little Turtle popped back up !!

"Great !" Little Turtle yelled to Coyote.
"This is where I live."

"Is itseeeeeeee !!!!" Iisaw yan hìngqawu.

Pam a'ni (hin'ur) itsivu'iwta.

Iisaw Yöngösonhoyat ahoy ngu'aniqe pam

paahut aqw tso'òmtit, pay pa'öymoki.

"Aaaaaaaaargh!!!!"   Coyote yelled.

He was very mad.

Coyote jumped into the water to catch

Little Turtle, and Coyote drowned.

43

Yaw yan Iisaw mooki.

Yaw panhaqam hinìwti.

Yuk pölö.

This is how Coyote met his end.

That's how it happened.

The end.

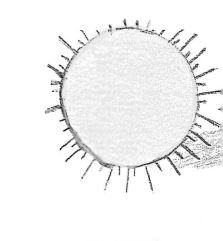

For Parents and Teachers:

Hopi is a vibrant and beautiful language. It has specific rules of grammar just as all languages do. These rules are quite different from English rules; however, it is these differences that make written Hopi fun and exciting to learn.

Here we offer just a few of the more simple points of grammar as an introduction to written Hopi, beginning with the all-important concept of Word Order. Examples are taken from the story to help with the explanations.

Additionally, Hopi is a combining language. To give more meaning to a word, Hopi speakers add letters or parts of words to the base word. A few examples of additions and how they are used are also given in the following pages.

Word Order

Hopi sentences use a different word order than English sentences. An English sentence is basically set up like this:

subject   verb   object

However, Hopi sentences are set up like this:

subject   object   verb

48

See the sentence on page 11.

In English:

The Turtles lived near Leenangwva.
  subject   verb   object

But when this same sentence is put into Hopi, it is written like this:

Yöngösosont Leenangwvat ep ki'yyungwa.
  subject   object   verb

(The small word *ep* implies the meaning "near.")

Articles

In English sentences, the articles *the*, *a*, *an* appear frequently. But in Hopi, there are no articles; they are only inserted when translating from Hopi to English. Examples of having to insert articles into English can be seen in numerous sentences in the story. Again, see the sentence at the top of page 11.

Yöngösosont Leenangwvat ep ki'yyungwa.

The Turtles lived near Leenangwva.

There is no word for *the* in the Hopi sentence; it is only implied. But when we write the sentence in English, we have to insert it. Not bothering with articles actually makes Hopi easier to write than English!

Tense Endings

Letters that mark the tense or "time" of a verb are added at the end of a Hopi verb.

Tense endings:

ni future tense: "will" do something

ngwu habitual tense: "usually do something"

Thus, the Hopi verb *tuuva*, "throw," becomes

tuuvani will throw

tuuvangwu usually throws

On page 35, Coyote says that he *will throw* Little Turtle into the Flute Spring if he does not sing:

"Um inumi qa tawlawqw, nu' ung Leenangwvami wiikye' ung aqw tuuvani," Iisaw kita.

"If you don't sing for me, I'll take you to Leenangwva and throw you in," Coyote said.

And the verb *maqnuma*, "hunt," becomes

maqnumni   will hunt

maqnumngwu   usually hunts

On page 13, see the sentence

Sutsep talavay Iisaw maqnumngwu.

Coyote also went hunting each morning.

(This was his "usual" morning activity.)

Some Other Useful Additions

Some additions tell the reader more about where something is, or where something is happening.

mi to, toward

q (adds distance, as in "way down")

See the sentence on page 39:

Little Turtle sank way down, poor thing.

Okiw, Yöngösonhoya atkyamiq pakima.

In this sentence, *atkya* means "below," or "underneath." With the additions of *mi* and *q*, *atkya* now means "way down below," or right at the bottom of the spring.

Marks That Describe Pronunciation Sounds

' A "stop." The voice stops its sound between two parts of a word, as in the English expression "uh-oh."

See sentence on page 13.

Now Coyote lived at Ismo'wala.

Yaw Iisaw Ismo'walpe ki'yta.

` A falling accent mark means that the voice falls in pitch on that syllable.

See sentence on page 27.

Then he saw Little Turtle under a bush.

Pàasat pam Yöngösonhoyat himutskit àasonngaqw tuwa.

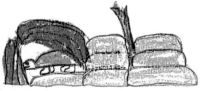

Often in Hopi, two letters are combined together to make one consonant sound. The kw in the word kwaahu, "eagle," is an example. But with the . separating the k and w, they become distinct sounds. The word kuk.wuwàaqe, to follow tracks, in the sentence on page 19 demonstrates this separation of sound between these two letters.

Pam as pumuy kuk.wuwàaqe amungkniqw a'ni (hin'ur) kotskiwa.

He tried to follow their tracks but the sand was too hot.

Men And Women Speak Differently

Men and boys at times use different words than women and girls do. For "thank you," men and boys say *kwakwhay*, and women and girls say *askwali*. In the story, on pages 14 and 15, the turtles find the sand <u>very</u> hot. Men and boys use the word *a'ni* to say "very" or "too," while women and girls use *hin'ur*.

Noqw sùutala'niqw, oovi a'ni (hin'ur) kotskiwa.

Since it was midsummer, the sand was very hot.

And finally, some words
are not translatable from
Hopi to English;
   Turtle's mournful song
   is a good example.

Tingawsona, tingawsona,

tingawsona, tingawsona,

Wa'ooo, wa'ooo,

Hi, hi, hi, hi !

Hopi to English Glossary

The following is a list of words that occur in this story. They are given meanings for the story here, but may have different meanings in other stories or general conversation.

A few nouns are listed in their objective form; see the section on word order for an explanation.

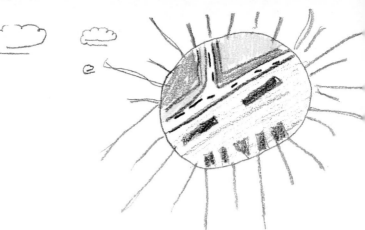

a'ni	very (used by male speakers)
àasonmiq	to a place underneath, to a place within
àasonngaqw	from beneath, from inside
ahoy	back, in return
akw	because of, by means of

ali	great!, good!
amungkniqw	after them
ang	along
aqle'	next to it
aqw	toward it, way into it
as	try to

atkyamiq	way down below
aw	toward it
ep	at, in, on
haqam	somewhere, where
haqamiya	they go somewhere
haqe'	along somewhere
hep	I already told you

hi	(a sobbing sound)
hìita	something, what
himu	someone, something
himutskit	bush, shrub (when used as an object)
hin'ur	very (used by female speakers)
hìngqawu	say something
hìngqawlawu	keep saying something, making sounds

Iisaw   Coyote

Iisawuy   Coyote
                   (when used as an object)

hinìwti   occur, take place

hìntingwu   usually happen in a
                        certain way

hisat   when, sometime, one time

iits   soon, early

inumi   for me, to me

is   (used to intensify the word that follows it)

Ismo'walpe   at the location known as Ismo'wala

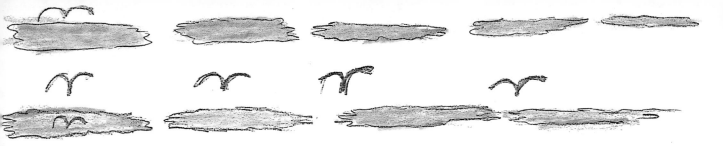

itse darn it! (an expression of frustration)

itsivu'iwta be angry

itsivuti get angry

ki'yta he/ she/ it lives, resides

ki'yyungwa they live, reside

kita said

kotskiwa   for the sandy ground to be hot

kotskiwqat   hot sand, hot ground (when used as an object)

kuk.wuwàaqe   follow tracks (from the verb *kuk.wuwa*)

kur   apparently, it seems

kuyva   appear

lasqe   turn off a path (from the
          verb *làasi*)

Leenangwvami   to Flute Spring

Leenangwvat   Flute Spring
          (when used as an object)

maqnuma   be hunting

maqnumngwu   usually be hunting

mooki	die
muumaniy	roll
natuwi'yta	accustomed to something
navota	hear
nawis'ew	finally
ngu'aniqe	will catch, will nab

ninma	they went home
niqw	when, and
noqw	it so happened
nu'	I
nuvat	snow (when used as an object)

nuy	me
Nuvatukya'oviy	Place of the Snow-capped Peaks (San Francisco Peaks, Flagstaff, Arizona)

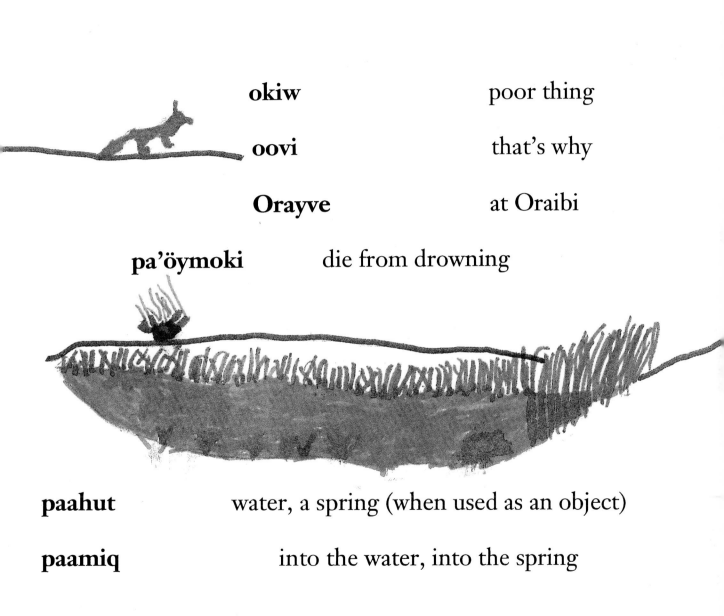

okiw   poor thing

oovi   that's why

Orayve   at Oraibi

pa'öymoki   die from drowning

paahut   water, a spring (when used as an object)

paamiq   into the water, into the spring

pàasat then, at that time

paki enter

pakima go in out of sight, sink

paklawu begin to cry, burst into tears

pakmumuya be crying

pam he, she, it

74

panhaqam   in that way

pante'   if it is to be that way

pay   well, now

pitut   after he/she/it arrived

piw   again

posvalweheheta   be bathed in tears

pölö   ending

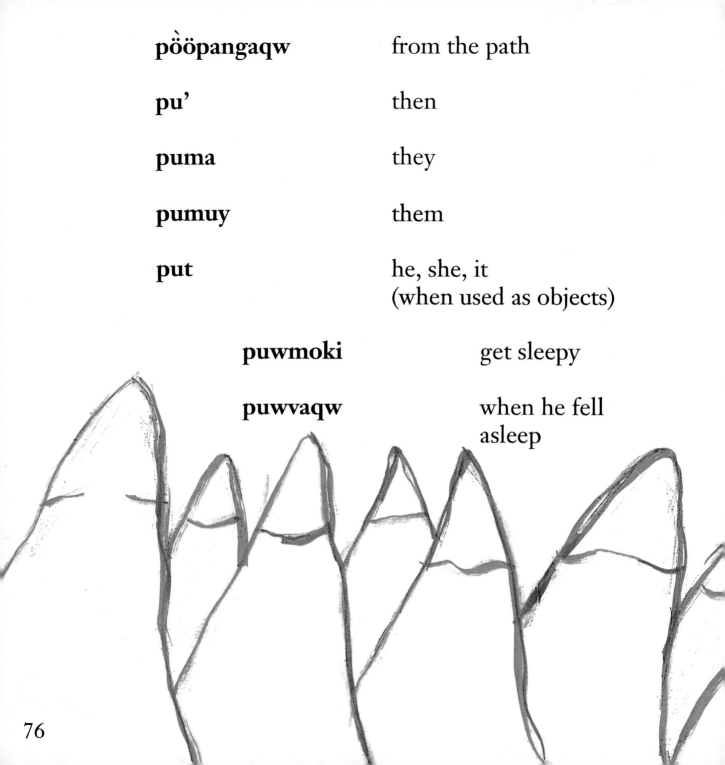

pòöpangaqw	from the path
pu'	then
puma	they
pumuy	them
put	he, she, it (when used as objects)
puwmoki	get sleepy
puwvaqw	when he fell asleep

qa	not
so'ni	oh no !

sòosoyam	all of them
sumokni	will quickly die
sutsep	each, every time
suukya	one

77

sùukyàatsantat   after grabbing quickly with the teeth

sùutala'niqw   since it was midsummer

taa'awu   that's okay

taatayi   wake up

talavay   morning

tawlawqw   while singing

tawlawuy   be singing

tawlawu'u   sing (a command)

78

taytaqw	while watching
tingawsona	(Turtle's lament)
töqti	call out
tso'òmtit	jump

tunöshepnumya   be looking for food

tunöshepnumyangwu   usually be looking for food

tuuva	throw
tuuvani	will throw
tuuwat	sand (when used as an object)
tuwa	find
um	you
ung	you (when used as an object)

wa'ooo (Turtle's lament)

wari run

wiikye' take along, bring

wuuwa think, wonder

wuuwanlawu keep thinking

ya (indicates a question)

yan this way

yangqw   from here, in here

yaw   it is said

yeesiwa   they were living

Yöngösonhoya   Little Turtle

Yöngösonhoyat   Little Turtle
(when used as an object)

Yöngösosont   Turtles

yuk   here, to this point

English to Hopi Glossary

Hopi is a context-sensitive language, wherein words take on different translations based on their usage.

Again, these words are given meanings for this story; they may have different meanings in other stories or in general conversation. This English to Hopi glossary is included here for purposes of cross-reference.

Nouns are listed in both [nominative], and [objective] cases; subjects of a sentence are in the nominative case, and objects are in the objective case. The [imperative] case indicates a command.

accustomed to something	natuwi'yta
after them	amungkniqw
again	piw
all of them	sòosoyam
along	ang
along somewhere	haqe'
angry (be angry)	itsivu'iwta
angry (get angry)	itsivuti
apparently	kur
appear	kuyva
arrived (after he, she , it ...)	pitut
asleep (when he fell ...)	puwvaqw
at, in, on	ep
at Ismo'wala	Ismo'walpe
at Oraibi	Orayve
back, in return	ahoy
bathed in tears (be ... ...)	posvalweheheta
beneath	àasonngaqw
(from ..., from inside)	
bush, shrub [nominative]	himutski
bush, shrub [objective]	himutskit

by means of, because of	akw
call out	töqti
catch (will ..., nab)	ngu'aniqe
Coyote [nominative]	Iisaw
Coyote [objective]	Iisawuy
cry (begin to ...)	paklawu
crying (be crying)	pakmumuya
darn it!	itse
die	mooki
die (will quickly ...)	sumokni
die from drowning	pa'öymoki
each, every time	sutsep
ending [noun]	pölö
enter	paki
finally	nawis'ew
find	tuwa
Flute Spring [nominative]	Leenangwva
Flute Spring [objective]	Leenangwvat
follow tracks	kuk.wuwàaqe

for me, to me	inumi
for sandy ground to be hot	kotskiwa
go somewhere (they ... ...)	haqamiya
grab quickly with the teeth	sùukyàatsantat

great!, good!	ali
happen (usually ... in a certain way)	hìntingwu
he, she, it [nominative]	pam
he, she, it [objective]	put
hear	navota

here (from ..., in here)	yangqw
here, to this point	yuk
home (they went ...)	ninma
hot sand [nominative]	kotskiwqa
hot sand [objective]	kotskiwqat
hunting (be hunting)	maqnuma
hunting (usually be ...)	maqnumngwu
I [nominative]	nu'
I already told you	hep

86

if it is to be that way	pante'
[an intensifier]	is
in that way	panhaqam
it, he, she	pam
it so happened	noqw
it is said	yaw
jump [verb]	tso'òmtit
Little Turtle [nominative]	Yöngösonhoya
Little Turtle [objective]	Yöngösonhoyat
living (they were ...)	yeesiwa
looking for food (be ... ...)	tunöshepnumya
looking for food (usually be ... ..)	tunöshepnumyangwu
me [objective]	nuy

morning	talavay
next to it	aqle'
not	qa
occur, take place	hinìwti
oh no!	so'ni
one	suukya
Oraibi [nominative]	Orayvi
Oraibi [objective]	Orayvit

path (from the ...)	pòöpangaqw
poor thing	okiw
[indicates a question]	ya
reside, (they live, dwell ...)	ki'yyungwa
resides (he, she, it ...)	ki'yta
roll	muumaniy
run	wari

San Francisco Peaks [nominative] (Place of the snow-capped peaks)	Nuvatukya'ovi
San Francisco Peaks [objective] (Place of the snow-capped peaks)	Nuvatukya'ovit
said	kita
sand [nominative]	tuuwa
sand [objective]	tuuwat
say something	hìngqawu
saying something (keep ... ...)	hìngqawlawu
she, he, it	pam
since it was midsummer	sùutala'niqw
sing [imperative]	tawlawu'u
singing (be ...)	tawlawuy
singing (while ...)	tawlawqw

sink, go in out of sight	pakima
sleepy (get ...)	puwmoki
snow [nominative]	nuva
snow [objective]	nuvat
[sobbing sound]	hi
someone, something	himu
something, what	hìita
somewhere, where	haqam

soon, early	iits
take along, bring	wiikye'
that's okay	taa'awu
that's why	oovi
them [objective]	pumuy
then, subsequently	pu'
then, at that time	pàasat

they [nominative]	puma
think, wonder	wuuwa
thinking (keep ...)	wuuwanlawu
this way	yan

89

throw	tuuva
throw (will ...)	tuuvani
to a place underneath, within	àasonmiq
toward it, way into	aqw
toward it	aw
try to	as
turn off a path	lasqe
Turtles [nominative]	Yöngösosont
Turtles [objective]	Yöngösosontuy

[turtle's lament]	tingawsona; wa'ooo
very [used by females]	hin'ur
very [used by males]	a'ni
wake up	taatayi
watching (while ...)	taytaqw
water, a spring [nominative]	paahu
water, a spring [objective]	paahut
water (into the ...)	paamiq
way down below	atkyamiq
well, now	pay
when, sometime, onetime	hisat
when, and	niqw
you [nominative]	um
you [objective]	ung